Mr Tick
the
Teacher

Ahlberg & Jaques

PUFFIN

PUFFIN BOOKS

UK | USA | Canada | Ireland | Australia
India | New Zealand | South Africa

Puffin Books is part of the Penguin Random House group of companies
whose addresses can be found at global.penguinrandomhouse.com.

www.penguin.co.uk   www.puffin.co.uk   www.ladybird.co.uk

First published in hardback by Viking and in paperback by Puffin Books 1981
This edition published 2017

001

Text copyright © Allan Ahlberg, 1981
Illustrations copyright © Faith Jaques, 1981
Educational Advisory Editor: Brian Thompson

The moral right of the author and illustrator has been asserted

Printed in China
A CIP catalogue record for this book is available from the British Library

ISBN: 978–0–141–36996–9

All correspondence to:
Puffin Books, Penguin Random House Children's
80 Strand, London WC2R 0RL

Tess Tilly Trixie

Mr Tick the teacher
lived in a big house
with his wife and children.
His wife's name was Mrs Tick.
The children's names were:
Tim, Tom and Teddy;
Tilly, Trixie and Tess.

Tom Tim Teddy

Mr Tick worked in a little school.
It was so little, it had only
one teacher – that was Mr Tick.
And it had only six children.
Can you guess who they were?

Every morning at half-past eight,
Mr Tick kissed Mrs Tick
and went off to school.
Every morning at ten to nine,
the children waved goodbye to Mrs Tick
and went off to school too.
At nine o'clock
the children lined up in the playground
and went into the classroom.

Then Mr Tick called the register.

"Tim!"

"Here, Daddy."

"Tom!"

"Here, Daddy."

"Teddy!"

"Here, Daddy."

"Tilly!"

"Not here, Daddy," said Tom.

"She forgot her dinner-money.

She went back to get it."

"Trixie!"

"Here, Daddy."

"Tess!"

"Here, Daddy."

After that the children
had their lessons with Mr Tick.
In the morning they had
reading, writing and arithmetic.
In the afternoon they had
singing, cooking and games.

At half-past three the children said
good afternoon to Mr Tick
and went home.
Mrs Tick was waiting for them
by the garden gate.
"Hallo, Mummy!" the children said.

"Hallo, Tim!
Hallo, Tom!
Hallo, Trixie!
Hallo, Tilly!
Hallo, Tess!" said Mrs Tick.
Then she said, "Where is Teddy?"
"He was cheeky to the teacher,"
said Tilly.
"Daddy kept him in."

So the days went by at the little school.

And they were happy days.

The children liked the teacher.

The teacher liked the children.

The parents were pleased with
the school.

The school was pleased with
the parents.

Then, one morning Mrs Tick
was reading the newspaper.
"Oh dear," she said. "Listen to this:
'LITTLE SCHOOLS MUST CLOSE
An inspector will visit
all little schools.
If a school does not have
enough children, it will
be closed down.
The children will go to a
bigger school.'"

"That's bad news," said Mr Tick.
"You children will lose a school,
and I will lose a job!"
"What we need is more children,"
said Mrs Tick.
"Yes," said Mr Tick. "But where from?"
All of a sudden Tilly said,
"I have an idea!"
She whispered it to Teddy.
"That's a good idea," said Teddy.
He whispered it to Mr Tick.
"That *is* a good idea," said Mr Tick.
He began to laugh.
"We will do it!"

We will
do it!

The next day the children
had some surprising lessons
in Mr Tick's class.
They had dressing-up lessons,

and making-faces lessons,

and riding-their-bikes-in-school lessons,
and eating-lots-of-dinners lessons.

Mr Tick took some old desks
from the school shed.
Mrs Tick put up more pegs
in the school cloakroom.
Can you guess what was going on?

Two days later, the inspector arrived.
Mr Tick met him at the school gate.
"The children are working in groups
this morning," he said.
"Come and see!"
Mr Tick took the inspector
round the school.

In the classroom he said,
   "Here we have the reading group."

In the playground he said,
   "Here we have the games group."

In the hall he said,
"Here we have the singing group."

On the school field he said,
"Over there we have the
cross-country running group."

Can you guess
who all the children were?
Well, the inspector could not.
He said, "This is all very good!"
And he put it down in his notebook.

At playtime the inspector had
a cup of tea with the secretary.
Can you guess who she was?
After play he saw some more groups.

Save me!
Save me!

At dinner-time Mr Tick took
the inspector into the hall again.
"Here the children are having
their dinners," he said.
"It is self-service."

Then the inspector had
a cup of coffee with the cook.
Can you guess who she was?

And he said,
"Well, Mr Tick, there is no need
to close *this* school.
You have plenty of children!"
Then he shook hands with Mr Tick
and said goodbye.

After that Mr Tick gave the cook
and the secretary a big kiss.
He gave the reading group,
the games group, the singing group
and the cross-country running group
a big hug.

And he gave a half-day's holiday
to the six cleverest
and most hard-working children
in the whole school.
And you can guess who they were!

The End